Hell's Press Presents

First paperback edition 2023

ISBN   978-1-7381321-3-3   (paperback)
ISBN   978-1-7381322-2-5   (ebook)

hellspress.com

Fairie Tales

The Three Little Pigs

COUNT FATHOM

Dedicated to...

.. you, who sweeps in front of her own
door. If there were many more, we
could keep the whole world clean. As
it is, there's far too few and the world
will stay much the way it's been. The
good cannot inflict the change upon the
cold and mean. The selfish will impose
their will and all the good demean.

And so it's said the dreams we have,
that they should not be small. For
if they are, and quiet too, the hoard
won't heed the call. The hearts of men
refuse to move, the weight is hard to
haul. What does it take to shake them
up, their minds to spark, enthrall?
Wise he was, he also said that we will
walk alone, those of us who beauty
see, who would choose to atone.

Johann Wolfgang von Goethe

Table of Contents

Preface

Affection is not out of place in this world. Abundant is love. We need time to unfurl a tapestry of woven fabric, fine in every way. A world in which one wanders, wonders, not alone.

Live in the valleys and vales of beyond, three little piggies , their whiskers still blond. Their mother, she dotes on them, has since their birth. But now she must yield to the turn of the earth. Piggies grow bigger as seasons roll by, and time comes when piggies from mother will fly in haste to a future they've dreamed of before,

with grandiose mansions and butlers
by doors.

Scheming and planning for future
to come, to danger and risk our piggies grow numb. Who is that lurking
about in the wood? I needn't tell you,
yet I think I best should. He's gracious,
you see now, in all the right ways, he's
cunning and guileful and tricky and
sleek, deceitful , deceptive, he preys on
the meek. Tenacious, I vow, you shan't
meet his gaze. His name is synony-
mous with none other than Nuck. But
I needn't tell you.

You've had the good fortune.

The Three Little Pigs

Let not this gruesome tale advise the reader to paint all creatures of a species with the same brush.

I, myself, once experienced a failing of this sort. I came upon a man so much like myself that I was stunned, and could not tell us apart, even under threat of death. My doppelganger, however, was suffering some emotional distress, as his face was contorted in anger, flushed red, with angry black squinted slits burning hateful, hidden eyeballs. It dawned upon me then that though we may be similar in countless ways, yet one should be careful mistaking between the two.

To my great surprise, at that very moment I became aware that, indeed, I was regarding myself, in a giant mirror where one was not expected. And I had a new revelation – that maybe characteristics are shared identically between us all, only varying in degrees. I've often thought so as I observed an insect closely and quickly understood his purpose, cheering him on in his task. And sometimes I've thought so as I reflect upon the fate of the pigs and the wolf in this very story.

A pig is much more easily understood than an insect, owing to our similarities.

Shelter and food, the need to feel loved, pigs share a great deal with the majority of mankind. Wolves, on the other hand, can only be understood by a select few. If you find yourself worried that you don't properly understand the nature of the wolf and cannot empathize with his predicament, I will do my utmost to show Wolfie in his best possible light, so as to alleviate your burden. Though that may prove difficult in this instance, as Wolf does little to recommend himself favourably. He's out to slaughter fat tasty pigs, after all.

Wolf had a long and noble reign as unquestioned monarch of the forests and dales and glens and ferns of the upper valley, even extending a goodly ways into the mountain terrain beyond. For nine long, generally peaceful, years the valley was protected from fearsome predators by our hero, that silver backed gentlemen meandering along. He clearly hasn't seen want for some time. What bravado! What style! What easy confidence, as he weaves an independent path across the land.

Unthreatened, Wolfie had the leisure to philosophize. With nothing to get terribly excited about day after day, Wolfie felt he had lost a little of the lust for life character-istic of his younger years. Sniffing out a doe hardly perked his ears for some time past. Now as the sun begins to set on his glorious career, Wolfie unfortunately let fall the rope.

What rope you might well ask. You should. Those of you pretending you know to which rope I am referring without me saying so directly are entertaining conjecture unworthy of the scholar. Enjoyable as it may be, one must remain disciplined and not jump to outrageous conclusions, even if you have unearthed evidence that well supports your claim.

For those of us not pretending to the scholarly, we can immerse ourselves in the world of interpretation, and approach the work free of all pretension, free to squeeze every last ounce of joy from the pages we clutch.

What rope, you might ask. The one we all hold in our hands. The tendency to ignore moral norms and pursue our pleasure down ethically dubious paths. The rope could be a leash, if you like, holding back an inner demon. Maybe it's not a rope after all, or any sort of thing like that. It's the real you being restrained, and the moral norms are a cage in which you are trapped. Maybe it's a ladder we climb towards moral purity, sliding down and breaking steps along the way in our ethical blunders.

Wolfie let go of a rope like that. His appetites began to stray into the abnormal. His perversions would worsen greatly in time, but for now he happened to have an unnatural taste for those three fat piggies growing handsomely on the outskirts of the village. At the appropriate age, these three were ready to set out on their own, leaving the warmth and safety of their childhood home to lay claim to some small portion of the world. Something they could call their own. Some stake they would plant, and maybe run up a little flag, announcing to the world that, yes, they were here and they mattered.

Dreams of a fat little piggy wife were indulged by all three. Her bending, tending the pot draped over the coals, little piglets running about, maybe one of the uncles playing a tune. A field of crops grows through the season, expertly managed by the shrewd hand of piggy, farmer savant.

Not one of them so much as glanced back at mother as her tears dropped on the lawn and she sadly waved a feckless trotter. She even fell to the ground in emotional collapse before they were out of sight. The ungrateful beggars couldn't give a tinkers toss. Such are the ways of youth. Not that these would have time to regret it.

Mother was overreacting, as usual. How far could a newly adult piggy get? They had already told her of the land that they had found, somewhat deeper into the forest, opening into a vast clearing, with a fresh vigorous stream running through, on which their hopes and dreams relied. With three of them keeping up filial appearances, her home would rarely be empty after all. Though it was, in fact, as only one piggy went home once in the following six month. It was pig Two. He didn't think he'd need a towel. But now he thought he'd rather have one, so he was going back to ask mother.

These three helpless little piglets did not yet comprehend the nature of the world, and strode confidently into the jaws of jeopardy. Our wolf may be slightly more rotund than you'd expect. But don't let that deceive you. Wolf was as wily as they come, and was yet to be out manoeuvred on his own terrain. Wolfie knew what was happening with those piggies, and recently he woke from a wet dream, even at his age, about that bacon.

Wolfie stalked out that clearing well, and in his addictively competitive way, wore out dozens of forest paths snaking through the surroundings, in preparation. He would mutter to himself, rehearsing interactions, agreeing, disagreeing, pleading, persuading, became irate with himself once or twice, and bumped into a tree, huffing eureka, nearly falling in the stream when finding the right words to complete his ditty:

Piggy, little piggy, let me come in! No?! Then I'll huff, and I'll puff, and I'll blow your house in!

Wolfie would tumble around in ecstatic laughter, wild eyes bulging and wet, then shut tightly in unendurable hilarity, gasping for breath.

Wolfie, having arranged his network of forest paths to his liking, moved off from the clearing he had named Piggy Trap, giving space and time for these three young oinkers to establish themselves on this ripe piece of real estate. Surely these piggies weren't so stupid as to not notice the smell of wolf in the vicinity. But, given time, they would be lulled into feeling secure. Wolf would let that time ripen further. In the fall, he would return to a triumphant and glorious feast on these three arrogant hams. Wolfie was off at a trot into the shadows of sunset.

I realize you don't know our piggies all that well at this point. Nor am I going to dive into the details of their upbringing, or their childhood experiences. That may be well and good, that you would clamour for some snippet or anecdote telling you more about each of the piggies, in your insatiable greed, your lust, your passion to know all. All you need know of the piggies will be told in this one character revealing tale.

Curious that despite all their other markings of civilization, like their adorable green patterned lederhosen, or their slightly German accent when they spoke English, their native language by the way, these pigs didn't actually have proper names, as you would well expect. They were simply called piggy number One, piggy number Two, and piggy number Three. They were the surviving three of a litter of thirteen, all these many years later. Best not to dwell on the fates of the others too much. Yes, some are interesting, and maybe more, one is extraordinary after all. But piggies One, Two, and Three are the focus of our tale.

They had received equivalent educations, were loved equally by their parents, shared equally in chores and community activities, and yet, as you will see, how very different could be the inclinations of these three little porkers. When, many years later, mother came to know of the doings and happenings of her little piglets, she was overcome with conflicting emotions, tearing her in one direction and the next. She suffered a psychotic collapse, and was rushed to hospital. She lived on another 26 months or so, but only as a shell of her former vivacious piggy self. She was listless and distracted, never quite recovering from the shock, and slowly slipped into the sorrow of eternal slumber.

On with the doings. Piggy number One was a slovenly disgrace of a pig. His mother would have been humiliated had she seen the filthy, dissolute life lived by her own loved little chopper. From day one in Piggy Glen, number One lazily propped a half bale of hay, tepee style, around the trunk of a fair sized deciduous in one corner of the clearing, and proceeded to lay about in the sun all day, rolling in the muck for some protection against the searing mid day heat. Never once did he deign to shuffle through the stream, even at the intimidating behest of his slightly more civil brothers.

Once the field work was undertaken, it must be said, piggy number One did his fair share and not without good humour. Some say piggy number One is the true philosopher of the bunch. Socrates would have approved, for piggy number One loved the company of all the living creatures of the valley, and would try to mate with any he could. His unrelentingly cheery demeanour softened the woes from all his failings and troubles. He contributed his fair share of the work, and he would thereby share in the spoils. How he arranged his finances was none of anyone's business. He was accused of, and in fact quite guilty of, low, some would say unacceptable, moral conduct on more than one occasion, once even meriting the attention of the local constabulary, whom duly made call at piggy number One's former residence and frightened his mother out of her wits for a day, until someone from the department called to reassure her that the peeping case had been put on the back burner as no one, herself included, quite knew where piggy number One was at.

Piggy number Two might look positively industrious next to his slothful brother number One, but I wouldn't give him a pass for his own adolescent delinquencies. Once again, none could fault this piggy for his field work. All participated and all were handsomely rewarded. Whatever number

One did with his income, no one could tell. He didn't seem attracted to wealth or luxury. His clothes could've been a tinkers second choice. Some secretly believe number One had amassed a fortune, and the treasure has never been recovered. Whole hobbyist clubs have been found out in pursuit round these parts. Whatever piggy number One had hidden in his closet, number Two was the opposite. He was an extrovert, and every blessed soul in the valley knew where his money went.

Piggy number Two was a thrill seeker, and a vain glory hunter. On any fine Tuesday in July, you might meet Two down at the zoo, paying extra to ride on a whale. Or a week Monday from thence, it's parachuting from a decommissioned military helicopter, sold off after the conclusion of some civil strife or other to a band of village baboons. Two was known to ring the bell and pay for rounds in a packed bar on Friday night, just to look the big pig for a moment. A fair surplus income was generated by the product of their labour, and yet Two was forever on his knees before his brothers, begging for mercy and swearing future fidelity to austerity.

Two was, of course, inclined to a bit more luxury than his lascivious monk of a brother. On the day of arrival he began work on a beachy bungalow at the stream's edge, with a deck out over the water. All wood, sanded down smooth, for he loved the sensual feel of sanded wood on his belly. Well.. the wood didn't end up all that smooth, for

Two was a better dreamer than a doer. The structure stood, provided shelter within and shade without. It would do for piggy Two, though his belly disagreed.

Over time, all but the barest of furniture had been pawned away. The allure of prestige and adventure proved all too tempting for poor piggy Two. He was weak, and he knew it, but he would defend himself hoof and jaw were you to abase him in any way. Two was left with his fine wood erection, that the creditors were sure to claim one day as compensation.

Which brings us to pig number Three, the sober one of the lot. Youngest by a mother's grunt, pig Three nevertheless exhibited a maturity far beyond that of his two worldly elder siblings. Pig Three had grasped the essence of responsibility prenatal. Were it not for piggy Three's meticulous preparation, the move to the clearing would have ended in tragedy.

Pig Three put a lot of time into digging the foundations for his quarters. For two harvests straight, pig Three dug diligently, and faithfully saved. Quarters for pig One were fully developed before the first moon rose, and little had improved since. Pig Two had more to do. But his carpentry was rudimentary, which limited his options. Trotters are not well adapted, so piggy Two had his jaws involved a lot, and what a sight it was. Using only saw, hammer, and nails, Two was lucky to have completed his structure before the first harvest.

After the second harvest, a day of glory was upon pig Three. A deep pit had been dug in a carefully measured rectangule, and proper framing shaped to receive the pour. In came wagons carrying barrels and bags of cement, and a queue of men to mix and pour in perfectly coordinated teams for the next seven and twenty hours, according to pig Three's calculations.

It's true, some of the men spat and bickered about doing business with these pretentious dwarves, these pot bellied farm animals. Most of the party shrugged and observed that pig money would keep the family fed. Some saintly few felt inwardly humiliated that they were being associated with those boorish peasants, and they re-solved to prove to the pigs that some men were enlightened, and went out of their way to pay respects to their employer. Rumour had it that pig One tried to mate with one of these type. Quite the hornet's nest of a debate was stirred over the actual results.

A fierce intensity of focus possessed pig Three for the day of the pour, a stress I needn't highlight for those that have felt the pressure. Pig Three had the workers colour coded and arranged in shifts. The pour came off well. One barrel slipped out of control as it was being mixed and spilled partially into the creek. Pig Three worked a miracle in the emergency, and sculpted a small bathing hole into the side of the stream with the spilled concrete. Two and thirty hours later, desperately exhausted, pig Three fell flat in the field, as the men gathered up their implements and shifted out with the wagons back to from whence they came, paid in full and marvelling at pig Three's superb management of the affair.

Pig Three came to under the shade of pig One's deciduous. There was a glass of water next to him. Soon his other brother noticed and came to help revive him and congratulate him on his impressive success. Now you may say that's not possible. But as you can plainly see, indeed it is. These pigs are not bit by jealousy. Pigs do not compete in some social hierarchy, where living standards and disposable income are the measure of worth, nor do they engage in dick measuring arguments. They knew whose dick was biggest, but so be it! To each his own, and the pigs lived in relative harmony.

Even the men on the pour were astonished by the pig social graces. They even tried to be more brotherly to one another as a result, and this in no small part is to be credited with the success of the operation. Though that social altruism subsided quickly enough back in the world of men. Poor Edgar, as they all said he let a pig mate him. That was mean, and not in the spirit of the pigs. Edgar denied this. But of course he would. The men knew what they had heard.

Pig Three came to under the deciduous, and, with his brothers, enjoyed mentally dressing the new concrete structure, careful to incorporate many positive elements of fengshui. Careful with those mirrors! Where do the plants go? They cleverly designed indoor plumbing around the stream, giving pig Three a sink, a toilet, and a shower, all according to principles of this foreign art. Yes, it would be nice. And you should have known it would be too. Doesn't Two's well sanded floor on which to rub your belly sound good? Pigs can be trusted with design elements. No! Remember pig one? Not all pigs can be trusted. See what I was saying earlier about the mirror? We're all pigs.

Time passed. The third harvest came in, and pig Three was well on his way, choosing a false brick look, solid dark wood trim, black out curtains on the bulletproof windows, and deck chairs by the pool. The pig pond, as they liked to say. Why bullet-proof windows? Pig Three was a paranoid sort, and security was an insurance policy as

he so often exclaimed. One day his theory
was put to the test.

We've been so concerned with the
doings of the pigs, that we have completely
neglected poor Wolfie, our would-be pi-
caresque protagonist. Yes, you know he's
waiting patiently for piggy plunder. But I've
asked you again and again to empathize with
the wolf, and your utter refusal frustrates
and confounds me. What do you think he's
doing out there in the wild? I'll tell you.

He has to protect that territory. And
he's no coward. He announces the extent
of his domain with scent, pissing over the
boundary of the lot of it with regularity,
let all comers try their luck, for Wolf was
keen for the fight. The territory is no palace
garden either, stretching league upon league

in all directions from Piggy Glen. The patrol kept Wolf lean and taut for his nine long years. Those who say he put on weight near the end weren't wrong. But remember he still had to eat.

Prey are not stupid. Prey are well adapted to escape even the wiliest of predators. But everyone slips up from time to time, and as an herbivore in this forest that could cost you your life. Wolfie liked prime rib, and he didn't fear the biggest bucks that had crossed this land in nearly a decade.

Wolfie was the law beyond the land of men. What you do in Wolfie's land, you do because he allows you to do it, a privilege he can revoke at his pleasure. Is Wolfie a tyrant? What do you think? He will kill. But only if he needs to, for sustenance or security.

So long as Wolfie is satisfied, then there is no fear in the forest. The leader does not demand unconditional loyalty, or threaten the innocent if they discover inconvenient truths, or red tape experimental, morally dubious, behaviour. Wolfie doesn't tell anyone what to think, and he doesn't stop anyone from saying what they like. He'd love it if you congregate! Throw wild parties and Wolfie will join in. Almost everyone will leave happy.

And you think it's that way because Wolfie lacks the conscious perspective of men? Ha! You racist. Wolfie is a hair's breadth of DNA from you. He could be your brother. But more likely you and your brother are pigs.

No, you are not the brother of a wolf because you haven't his refinement. He is an more noble lord than any I've met. He wields the sceptre with the impartiality of death incarnate. On the land of the wolf, the law benefits the best. All hail, Wolfie. And he's coming for those pigs.

Throughout these months of harvest and seed, Wolf frequented, when time allowed, the tangle of paths surrounding the clearing. He soon came to know those that the pigs used regularly, their habits and comings and goings. He knew every aspect of their lives, and had prepared a psychological portfolio on each and their expected response to critical pressure. He knew that pig Three was an opponent to seriously respect. More in the denouement on Wolfie's portfolio. Wolf bides with religious patience the pass of seasons, choosing his climax with care.

It was an hoary November 9th, a Tuesday the records show, when Wolfie descended on the glen for the piggy feast. What few leaves were left attached after the recent howling of the winds were fading quickly to an arid brown. There was no hiding on the paths. Now, I know your sceptical mind will immediately react. If this plan is so well thought out, then why does Wolfie go for pig number One first? It makes no sense. Get the hardest pig out of the way, and take up residence in that fortress of a house before easily sweeping up One and Two. And again, you disgust me. You're not a wolf.

This is a wolf at the tail end of an illustrious career. Now is the time for his requiem mass. This is not some sneaky shuckster robbing a boy of a nickel. This is Wolf! His plan was Herculean in nature, each labour exceeding the magnitude of the last. Wolf was going to sign his name to his deed of life with this act of poetry. He trotted out of that forest with brazen confidence.

Wolf almost broke character on his way up to the deciduous, though. A bulge eyed wild smile danced across his face for a moment. He quickened his pace and stopped dead in front of One's tree and blurted out the hilarity:

"Piggy, little piggy, let me come in! I'll huff and I'll puff and I'll blow your house in!"

Wolfie lost it completely. He collapsed on the ground, rolling about, in joyous agony for some moments. They were just the moments piggy One needed to shoot out of the hay like a young rabbit from a triste with the farmer's daughter when the porch light clicks on. He was across the clearing and ensconced in Two's bungalow in just a panting dog's breath, well before Wolf had pulled himself together. Wolf proceeded in his theatricals none the wiser.

"Get yourself out of that hay, you fat porker, right this second, and go for a run. I'm going to chase you down and tear the soft flesh from your living body with my ca-nines. Soon enough I'll do the same to your two brothers, and I hope they're listening! I am Wolf, and everyone pays their due at some point or other. Your bill is due today, piggy One."

Pig One cowered with Two in the beach bungalow as they listened to the speech, breathless in fear and horrified anticipation. Pig Three, funnily enough, busied himself with paper and kindling in the fireplace.

Wolfie eventually scattered the hay, and, to his dismay, his shock and surprise, the cunning little porker had disappeared. Wolf had carefully surveyed the field before his grand entrance, and somehow the plump little snack had made the scoot.

Furious at this failure in the first eight bars of his piece, Wolfie chased his tail thrice and gave his head a shake. Then he stood stalk still and stared blankly a moment, a method tried, tested and true to calm and focus our hero. Wolfie pranced maniacally over to his favourite property, the bungalow. This simple wooden structure showed some respect for the natural world, providing for one's necessities without unduly damaging the surrounding land. One should blend into the nature, not try to subdue it. Wolf and this pig shared a dao outlook, without spiralling into One's extremism.

"Listen, you fat heffers! I'm going to rip off your hindquarters and eat them in front of you while you draw your last breath! Your panicked squeals will accompany my bloody feast! This is a message to all in the forest, that the fortunes of fate are finicky, and do not pay obeisance to any of the illusions of fairness and equity you so cherish!

Doom is the eventual fate of all, and you will not be an exception." Listen and reflect on the story of the three little pigs.

Without waiting for a reply, Wolfie pulled out a handy flint he kept and busied himself snapping sparks at the base of the bungalow. Wolf wouldn't be able to keep his promise if the pigs roasted, but literal truth was rather beside the point, as just the threat appealed to Wolfie's poetic soul. The more he thought about it, Wolf was happy with the way things were going. He was actually glad pig One made his mad dash to an illusory safety. The best laid plans of mice and men, after all, come to nought. This small alteration made for a grand finale with a three-on-one showdown at the fortress. Wolfie nearly wet himself again at the thought, and struck his flint with such enthusiasm that the conflagration flared up in a twinkle.

How did the two trapped pigs react? Well, pig Two was little help at all. He had browned his lederhosen, curled up fetal, and whimpered a second puddle, of tears this time, to the floor. Pig One, shook badly by the Wolf's arrival, had regained possession of himself by now. He gave Two a good butt in the belly, a nip on the ear for encouragement, and led Two in a race, despite his misgivings about cleanliness, down into the creek, through Three's pool, and into the concrete castle while Wolfie tossed and spun in delight as the flames swarmed ever higher.

Three thrust what would have been a fist had he fingers forward as One and Two once again eluded the lunacy of the wolf.

One had to admit Wolf was, at this point, taking his character maybe a little too far. Or was it so? Seize the day! This was Wolfie's last moment of grandeur. A dramatic bow as the curtain falls. A triumphant Wolf would leave a lasting impression, etching his name into stone annals of fable lore for all time.

Pigs One, Two, and Three holed up and prepared for a siege. That wolf wasn't getting in. No way, no how. Pig Three was, among other things, an avid reader of Napoleonic war strategy, and an itchingly paranoid fellow to boot. Doors and windows were barricaded. The water intake was too narrow for wolf. Maybe a fox could fit through, but not Wolfie. The same could be said for the thoughtful slits pig Three had designed, like arrow shoots in a castle tower, for better air circulation. A sparrow might well playfully and enjoyably penetrate, but not a wolf. Then there was the fireplace.

Hmm... That was a problem, and, as we've seen, piggy Three had the fire roaring well in time for Wolfie's attack. Three had planned for a proper mechanical flue to control air flow around the fire, but sadly the Wolf had arranged his attack before pig Three was prepared. Napolean had gained a night's march on him. But he wasn't about to buckle. Not yet. The fire will keep Wolf from the door. For now.

"I'm not the idiot you imagine, little pigs. I see that smoke billowing from the chimney top. You are my magnum opus. You should be proud to play the sacrifice upon the alter in my illustrious farewell!"

Wolfie filled his prodigious lungs with air, braced himself with exuberant pride, and belted out with a ferocious joy, "Little piggy, Little piggy, let me come in!"

Pig Three's furrowed brow showed respect for the solemnity of Wolfie's moment. There was a suspenseful pause, pregnant with possibility. Pig Three cupped his trotter about the lower portion of his piggy face, stroking a moment gently, drew in what air he could, and in his stressed, shaking soprano, tooted "Not by the hairs of my chinny chin chin!"

Pig Three was sharply stung with instant regret. All three pigs felt utterly and hopelessly lost at that exact moment. What a blunder. Pig One summed it up perfectly.

"That line really Nucked us."

Wolf was, at that moment, running a hose from the creek up to the roof of the house. He was halfway up a ladder... Hey! Yes, he prepared for all of this, hiding things throughout the tangled paths surrounding the clearing according to his research of likely outcomes. He heard Three's silly response, delivered in a panicked, dramatic form, the frightened pitch of a pig before the slaughter. But the defiance in his voice was notable, and one could discern true courage lay beneath what his fearful emotions would betray. Then Wolfie knew. He was destined to be a legend.

On the roof, next to the chimney stack, Wolfie took a fairly broad stance, threw back his shoulders and his head, filled his chest to capacity, and with a well practiced rhythm, modelled after ripples in a pond from a thrown stone, delivered his masterpiece:

"Then I'll huff!" A brief silence as Wolfie gasps for air.

"And I'll puff!" Wolfie's bass lowered perceptibly, as did the omens of evil intent veiled in his intonation, followed by the coup de grace, crackled in a demented rage:

"And I'll blow......... your house.... in!"

Once more Wolf sacrificed truth, which he found inflexible and unaccommodating, for dramatic appeal. Nevertheless, his accomplishment is to this day unsurpassed. From a full story and a half high, Wolf sucked up enough water from the creek, blowing it forcefully down into the fireplace, and eventually, after immense inimitable effort, quenched all the flames beneath, flooding a thumb of the first floor in his labour.

Yes, I've heard many say this feat is impossible. Sucking water up a pipe to the height of a story cannot be done. I'm not going to persuade you of the veracity of events as I've related them. They were told to me by the very Wolf that performed them, for a task is worth nothing if not related said the Wolf. Far worse when it is not related well, and is therefore not appreciated. An old Wolf on his way out of the world record-ed his legacy, for all to ponder the worth of the Wolf and his ways.

The pigs within could not be charac-terized as a group anymore. We may share our joys, but our sorrows are ours alone. Pig Three dashed to and fro pulling drawers from their slots, banging cupboard doors, rummaging closets in wild desperation, and when he finally opened the fridge with one last dolorous hope, pig Three finally broke down and crumpled to the floor in a piggy heap, squealing for mercy from the heavens.

Pig Two was an oddity. Though I suppose, with all three reacting differently and no comparable situation from which to collect a data set and make predictions, then each one must be considered an oddity. Perhaps I am the oddity for thinking so, as the wolf, when relating the matter, proposed no special significance to pig Two's reaction. You can let me know. Pig Two, hyperventilating at first, calmed himself down to a manageable degree. He was an adult after all. Two sunk slowly to the floor, dragged himself stutteringly, as one side of him was inexplicably and unexpectedly paralyzed, across the floor into a corner. Once there, piggy Two curled right up fetal, like an enormous sweaty flesh bagel and whimpered softly for mommy between piteous bouts of quiet, but violent, rhythmic sobbing.

Pig One was composed. He had been sitting still since he arrived sparkling from the dash in the creek. Pig One was clean. His mind felt clear. Pig One understood that sooner or later that, in his opinion, black-hearted devil would slip down the chute, and the three pigs were utterly and hopelessly doomed. He reasoned further that, indeed, we were all so since the moment of our birth. The wolf will come and tear us mercilessly from our flesh. He is the shadow under which we burn as the briefest of candles. And he is the reason our light is necessary. Pig One bowed comfortably down, chin on trotters before the mantle, and enjoyed the coral of ideas dazzling his mind with death so near upon him.

The Wolf had carried the game to its grizzly conclusion. Some will savour each syllable, twirling it round on the tongue to taste its meaning. Some abhor gore. Posterity demands we bare our nakedness.

Down the chimney the wolf slipped, quick as a switch. He emerged within a true monster, and tore each squealing frightened pig to pieces, bathing the floor and walls and ceilings in blood, red himself from tip to tail, pig limbs asunder in a scatter across the room, and finally, shaking the clouds high in the heavens with a mighty howl of pride and fulfillment, echoing to this very day in the canon lore of Fairie Tale.

The End

Acknowledgments

The authors that have led the way, the rebels that rebel. Friends and family have I called out in acknowledgment as well. But one most precious waits within my heart. Her thanks I'll stand and tell.

Once I was a vagrant, traipsing lone across the land, till you caught me on my travels, stopped me, took me by the hand. Now, forever more, your lightest wish is my command. Once I was a fishy, swimming lost in oceans wide. You caught me in your net and magic potion you applied. Now if asked I'd swim in fire, and for you my death abide. Once I was a mongrel, without a home, without a place. You came and took a hold of me, and leashed me just in case. Now we are together, and no force can ever part. My days are yours forever, as hand and paw are interlaced.

Helen, you are something that my words cannot define, a magic creature hid amongst us, you're an omen, you're a sign. You have loved and you have tortured, you have changed my blood to wine. You are all, and ever with me, every thought I have is thine.

Author

Love is a word that defies explanation. Source, if you will, it's effect or causation. Find, you will not, to eternal frustration. But yet it's a word known across every nation. Follows it not any rules of gestation. What is it then? Flirtation? Elation? Why does it suffer such frequent fluctuation? What are the ingredients it needs for creation? It seems not to need any solid foundation, but springs up unaware, like a monstrous mutation. Your heart feels a sudden unexpected palpitation. Will it last? Is it true? Does this love have duration? The answers, while sought, cause a burning vexation. I'll say what I know, not a lot, in ovation. Love is a kind of spiritual dilation.

Love is attached at the hip, for this man, with duty, obligation to fulfill a demand. It's not just a word, but more like a gland. Love compels action, don't misunderstand. Do, you must, if in love you trust, all that you can, whether moral or not, for love is not above a touch of slight of hand. A paralyzed love deserves reprimand. In some places and ways love's considered contraband. But not here. Here in abundance you can find love, in the land of the Fairie Tale..

Hell's Press

In a prison does a man reside and while away his hour. Brief, it is, and stained, it won't wash off within the shower. Share the time, he does, with men who seek and abuse power. Lock himself away, he would, in far and lofty tower. Avoid the plague of men, he should, whose offerings are sour. A wife he needs, like Helen, my rare and trasured flower.

9 781738 132133